THE
MILLION DOLLAR
POTATO

THE MILLION DOLLAR POTATO

BY
LOUIS PHILLIPS

ILLUSTRATED BY
GEORGE ULRICH

SIMON & SCHUSTER
BOOKS FOR YOUNG READERS

Published by Simon & Schuster
New York · London · Toronto
Sydney · Tokyo · Singapore

SIMON & SCHUSTER BOOKS FOR YOUNG READERS
Simon & Schuster Building, Rockefeller Center,
1230 Avenue of the Americas, New York, New York 10020.

SIMON & SCHUSTER BOOKS FOR YOUNG READERS
is a trademark of Simon & Schuster
The text of this book is set in 14 pt. Sabon.
The display type is Camelot.
The illustrations are pen and ink.
Designed by Vicki Kalajian
Manufactured in the United States of America

10   9   8   7   6   5   4   3   2   1

Library of Congress Cataloging-in-Publication Data
Phillips, Louis.   The million dollar potato / by Louis
Phillips ; illustrated by George Ulrich.   p.   cm.
Summary: An eight-year-old boy inherits a million dollars
on the condition that he spend the same amount in twenty-four
hours.   [1. Inheritance and succession — Fiction.] I. Ulrich, George, ill.
II. Title.   PZ7.P54Mi   1991   [Fic] — dc20   90-49832

ISBN 0-671-67207-X

for
ELIZABETH BERGER
OONA CURLEY
RACHEL KAUFMAN
WILLIAM LURIE

CONTENTS

CHAPTER 1

TIMOTHY INHERITS A MILLION DOLLARS IN FIVE DOLLAR BILLS

No doubt you have already heard the story of the eight-year-old boy named Timothy Watt who lived in the small town of Butrum Molasses, California. And no doubt you have heard what happened to him when he inherited a million dollars in five dollar bills from his Great but eccentric Aunt Jessica. But even if the story has been well reported on television news programs, many details have been left out. I shall try to fill them in as we go along.

At age three, Master Timothy, who had been living in an orphanage on the edge of town, had been adopted by his Great and eccentric Aunt Jessica. Aunt Jessica was very rich but very lonely. Thus her great-nephew Timothy was a great comfort to her in her old age. They frequently went on long walks together around the green lawn of Great Aunt Jessica's mansion. Great Aunt Jessica would point out all the different flowers and plants that grew upon her estate, and together they took great delight in feeding the many swans that floated on the private pond. Aunt Jessica even kept two great snowy owls in her bedroom.

But one day, when she was ninety-four years old, Great Aunt Jessica died. She left her owls to the Butrum Molasses Bird Sanctuary, and to her beloved nephew she left one million dollars in five dollar bills.

Thus it happened that on one Saturday morning, after Timothy had been watching fourteen hours of cartoon shows, he was instructed to meet with his great aunt's lawyers. When Timothy walked downstairs and saw the five dollar bills stacked up to the ceiling, he could not believe his eyes.

"Now all this money has been left to you by your Great Aunt Jessica," one of the lawyers said. "But she also left you some instructions."

"You will receive the one million dollars only if you promise to spend the entire sum within twenty-four hours after receiving it," a second lawyer added.

"You must also spend the entire million dollars in one place," a third lawyer said. "And you can buy only one thing with it."

Timothy gulped. "I have to spend all that money within twenty-four hours, in one place, and just buy one thing?" He took off his baseball cap and scratched his bright-red hair. It sounded like a difficult task.

"If there was one thing your Great Aunt Jessica could not stand, it was frittering. Your great aunt did not want you to fritter away a million dollars little by little, penny by penny, dollar by dollar. You can buy anything your heart desires. Any one thing that costs exactly one million dollars. Not a penny more, nor a penny less."

The Lawyer-in-Charge held out a gold pen. "If you agree to the terms, just sign your name."

Timothy gulped. Naturally it was a very difficult decision for an eight-year-old boy to make — especially a boy who had been raised in isolation upon a great estate. So he decided to consult his only friends — the two snowy owls that were kept in Aunt Jessica's very cold, almost frozen bedroom.

"Who?" asked the owls when Timothy opened the door.

"Watt," answered Timothy, saying his last name.

"Who? What?" said the owls, annoyed that they were being awakened in the middle of the day.

"I need to know what to do. Should I accept the money?" Timothy asked. But of course the owls, about to be taken off to the Bird Sanctuary, could only blink at him.

"Don't be foolish," the butler said. Jacques, the sixty-year-old butler, had followed Timothy into the bedroom. "You should make your Aunt Jessica happy by agreeing to her wishes."

Then the lawyers walked in, and the lawyers talked and talked and talked. Finally Timothy gave in. He signed his name at the bottom of the papers.

"I'm just a little boy," Timothy thought. "What am I going to do with a million dollars?"

"It is now seven P.M., Saturday, August 17th," said the lawyers. "You have exactly twenty-four hours, or until seven P.M. tomorrow evening to make your purchase." The lawyers put on their hats, picked up their briefcases, and left Timothy alone with the servants and butlers in the great big house to contemplate his future. "Remember! You can only buy one thing."

Timothy, having no time to waste, ran outside, jumped upon his bicycle, and pedaled furiously into the center of Butrum Molasses. The great clock that shone over City Hall said eight o'clock. Timothy had only twenty-three hours left.

CHAPTER 2

THINGS GET WORSE AND WORSE AND WORSE

But all the stores were closed. And tomorrow would be Sunday!

CHAPTER 3

TIMOTHY MEETS A VERY STRANGE OLD WOMAN

Timothy parked his bike and started to walk. As he walked, he thought, and as he thought, he walked. He walked and thought, and thought and walked, but all the stores were still closed. Time was running out.

Timothy turned down a narrow alleyway that ran along the rear entrance to the Mystic Hardware Company. At the end of the alley, there were four green doors and a row of windows set into a brick wall. These doors seemed to indicate a row of small apartments. In one window a light was burning.

Timothy stopped running and peered inside. He saw a white-haired woman in a long, black flowing robe. She was bent over a small kettle in a fireplace. The sight startled him. He didn't know that anyone lived in the alley. Timothy had just about decided to go away and not bother the woman when the door suddenly opened. A woman with a long nose and a deeply wrinkled face said, "Well, what brings the likes of you to my door at this time of night?"

Timothy quickly removed his red baseball hat. "Please, miss, I didn't mean to disturb you. But you see my name is Timothy Watt."

"Yes, you're the young man who has inherited a million dollars, but you have to buy one object with it, one thing that costs a million dollars."

Timothy was taken aback. "How could you possibly know that?"

"Oh, I have my ways." The old woman cackled. "So I ask you again. What brings you to my door at this time of night?"

"I was hoping that there was a store in this alley, a store where I could buy something."

"Well, there is no store in *this* alley." The old

woman cackled again. "But come inside. Maybe I can be of help."

Timothy entered the tiny apartment and the old woman latched the door. There was not much furniture in the room. Timothy saw a narrow cot with a dark gray cat upon it. There was a bookcase filled with books of strange shapes and colors. And there was a single table with a raw potato resting on top. A black kettle boiled in the fireplace.

"If you are hungry," the old woman said, "I am making stew. You can eat that if you wish."

"No, thank you," Timothy said as politely as he could. The dark gray cat curled itself around Timothy's pant leg.

"Nono!" the old woman scolded her cat. "Leave our guest alone. He has a big problem to solve and no time to play games." She pointed toward the narrow cot. "Please sit down," she said, "and tell me your problems."

Timothy sat down and told her all about his Great Aunt Jessica and her strange gift.

"I guess your great aunt wanted to test your character," the old woman said.

"My character?" Timothy asked. "But I'm going to lose all that money!"

"Well, you haven't lost it yet." She took some stew from her kettle and held the ladle to Timothy's lips. "Here, taste this. You're probably very tired and hungry."

"Thank you, but I am not very tired. And I'm not very hungry." But after he had taken just three sips of the woman's delicious stew Timothy felt the room start to spin. He thought he heard the cry of bats and the hissing of snakes. He placed a hand to his forehead. It was dripping with sweat. "The old woman's crazy!" he thought. "She's a witch. I've been poisoned by a witch."

"Yes, everybody thinks entirely too much about money," the old woman said, her eyes gleaming. "People buy and sell, sell and buy things that have absolutely no worth. They forget what is truly important in life. But you, my boy, will not forget. I promise that you will be different from the others."

She laughed, and Timothy collapsed to the floor in a faint.

CHAPTER 4

A MILLION DOLLAR POTATO

When Timothy awoke, he found himself lying on a narrow cot covered with a heavy wool blanket. He rubbed his eyes and sat up. "Where am I?" he asked. The black cat named Nono jumped onto his cot.

"Why, you are here — quite safe and cozy with me," the old woman said. Outside, bells from the church started to ring. The sound reminded him of his need to make haste. "Do you know what time it is?" he asked. "I have a very important errand to accomplish before seven o'clock Sunday night."

"Then you don't have much time. It's already a quarter to seven."

"In the morning?"

"Oh, no, young man. You've slept away almost all of Sunday. It's a quarter to seven . . . in the evening."

"In the evening?" Timothy looked alarmed. "I have only fifteen minutes left to buy something for a million dollars. If I don't buy something, I'll lose my inheritance."

Time was running out.

"Maybe you have something you would want to sell me," he suggested.

"For a million dollars?" The old woman laughed.

"I'll buy your cat!" Timothy exclaimed.

The old woman shook her head. "Not Nono. Some things are beyond price. Sit down and I'll make you some potato soup." She picked up a potato.

"I'll buy that!" Timothy shouted. "I'll give you a million dollars for that potato." He turned to look at the clock on the wall. The hand on the antique clock moved ever so slightly. It was now

26

6:59. There was just one minute left!

"With a million dollars you could get a lot more potatoes than one," the old woman said. She started to laugh with a high-pitched cackle.

"Please!" Timothy begged. "Please let me buy that potato!"

"All right," the old woman said. "If you want it so much."

Timothy sank onto the cot and breathed a sigh of relief. "I'll have the money delivered to you tomorrow morning. But I'll need a bill of sale."

"Very good," the woman said, but Timothy could not tell if she believed him or not. The old woman wrote out a bill of sale.

CHAPTER 5

A VERY UNPLEASANT SURPRISE

Timothy bade the old woman and her cat farewell, jumped on his bicycle and pedaled home as fast as he could. Aunt Jessica's lawyers were waiting for him.

"Well, did you buy something?" the lawyers asked.

Timothy held his potato out proudly. "This is what I've bought."

"You mean you've bought a potato farm?" the Lawyer-in-Charge asked. "Now there's a good investment."

"No, sir. I have just bought this one potato here."

"One potato for a million dollars?" The lawyers turned pale.

Timothy nodded, and showed them the bill of sale.

The lawyers shook their heads in disappointment. "Well," the Lawyer-in-Charge told the others, "the bill of sale looks official enough, but Master Timothy has squandered one million dollars with nothing to show for it. What a waste. A tragic waste!" They instructed the butler to call for the chauffeur to start their limousine.

Timothy watched as the lawyers drove away. Then he carried his potato to the dining room, but when he entered the room he received the shock of his life. All the five dollar bills had disappeared!

Timothy looked high. Timothy looked low. Timothy ran from room to room. He questioned the butler and the servants and the gardener. But not a single bill could be found. Someone had stolen the entire million dollars. Timothy lay down on his bed and cried and cried. He thought he must be the most unhappy eight-year-old in the entire world.

"Now what am I going to do?" Timothy wondered. "I promised the old woman that I would bring her the million dollars by tomorrow morning and now I have only . . . " Timothy stopped, emptied his pockets. He had only 78¢. He was $999,999.22 short. Timothy was now in a worse plight than before. He decided to bicycle back to Mystic Alley and tell the old woman what had happened. Perhaps she would forgive him. But first he called the police to tell them about the theft.

CHAPTER 6

IN SEARCH OF THE STRANGE OLD WOMAN

Timothy bicycled to the alley next to the hardware store. But when he looked for the old woman's apartment, he found that the window had been boarded over.

"Old woman," he called. "Yoo-hoo." But there was no reply. A note on the door read:

> Dear Timothy,
> Please take care of Nono
> for me. I have to go away
> to London to help other
> young persons in distress.
> Be brave.
> All shall be well.

Timothy carefully removed the note. When he stepped back, he felt something soft against his ankles. He glanced down and there was the gray cat—Nono. .

"Nono? Is that you?" He quickly picked up the old woman's cat and gave it a friendly pat. "Where is your owner?" he asked. Nono purred.

Timothy looked and looked, but the old woman was nowhere around. So he decided to take Nono home. Perhaps the old woman would come looking for him.

On the following morning, Timothy poured himself some orange juice, poured some milk into a saucer for Nono, and then sat down to read the morning paper — *The Butrum Bugle and Daily Molasses*. As soon as Timothy saw the huge headlines, he groaned. In huge black letters *The Butrum Bugle* proclaimed to all the world:

PAYS $1,000,000 FOR A HOT POTATO

The news story explained how a foolish boy by the name of Timothy Watt had squandered his inheritance by buying one single potato.

By late afternoon Timothy's name had been

mentioned on every television and radio news show. Reporters gathered on the front lawn to take his picture.

Timothy's phone refused to stop ringing. All day and night people kept calling to tell him how stupid he was and what they would have bought if they had had a million dollars.

Nono fled under the bed. And when Timothy finally fell asleep, he dreamed about a potato that was larger than the entire earth. The largest potato in the universe.

CHAPTER 7

A VERY PLEASANT SURPRISE

Timothy was so unhappy that he stayed in bed for two whole days. On the morning of the third day, the doorbell rang. Timothy decided to answer it.

When he opened the door, a tall, pale-faced man dressed in a tuxedo said, "Hello. My name is William C. Hagstrom. I have come to look at that potato of yours. May I see it?"

"Certainly." Timothy went to his aunt's desk and pulled out the potato. It was wrapped in a plastic bag tied with a bright yellow ribbon. The man took the bag and held it up to the light.

"Very beautiful," he said. "You obviously have the eye of a connoisseur."

"Connoisseur?"

"One who collects rare art objects," Mr. Hagstrom explained. "And now you have collected the rarest art object of them all. I dare say that there is only one potato in the whole world that is worth a million dollars and you own it. Do you realize, young man, how many collectors there are in this world who will gladly give more than a million dollars for your investment? I personally represent a client who is prepared to give you a certified bank check for *two* million dollars for this potato."

Timothy could hardly believe his ears. Here was a man prepared to offer him two million dollars for a potato.

"Well, young man. What do you say?" Mr. Hagstrom waved the check under Timothy's nose. Nono mewed.

Timothy thought a moment. Then he shook his head. "I don't want to sell it quite yet. I just bought it and it isn't quite paid for."

"No problem. You'll pay for it when I pay you,"

said Mr. Hagstrom, You're a good businessman."

"But I don't want to sell it," Timothy said.

The man looked extremely displeased. "Sell the potato, you little brat!"

"This is a free country. I don't have to sell it if I don't want to."

"All right. But you'll be sorry you turned my client down. I'll tell the whole world." And with that, the man in the tuxedo stalked out of the house and slammed the door. Nono mewed.

Timothy and Nono were alone again.

Soon newsboys all over America were shouting out the latest news: "Extra! Extra! Read all about it! Timothy turns down two million dollars for his potato. Art collectors clamor for a glimpse of the two million dollar spud."

No doubt about it. The million dollar potato — now the *two* million dollar potato — was fast becoming the most talked about object in the world.

As Nono and Timothy tried to decide upon a course of action, the doorbell rang again. There at the door stood Captain Herman Menes, chief of the Butrum Molasses police force. With him was the old butler, Jacques. Captain Menes had his prisoner handcuffed.

"I just thought I'd let you know," the police captain said, "that we have caught the man who stole your million dollars. This is Frank 'the Brain' Schneider, a famous thief. Do you recognize him?"

Timothy nodded. "I certainly do. But we called him Jacques."

Nono mewed.

"We caught him when he tried to open a bank account. The serial numbers on the five dollar bills matched the numbers given to me by your Aunt Jessica's lawyers. They are quite scrupulous when it comes to keeping track of such things."

The police captain pointed to his van, which was stuffed with five dollar bills. "I believe those belong to you."

Timothy's pulse quickened. A big smile spread across his face. He was happy to get Aunt Jessica's money back. Now he could pay the Old Woman what he owed her.

"Thank you," he said. "Thank you very much!"

"Think nothing of it." Captain Menes led Frank "the Brain" away. Outside the gates of Aunt Jessica's estate, a large group of men, women, and children had gathered. They cheered when they saw Timothy. "Show us the two million dollar potato," they chanted. "Show us the two million dollar potato."

Timothy brought the potato forward and held if aloft. A great cheer went up from the crowd. "Hurray for Timothy!" they cried.

The noise and chanting and cheering continued until late in the night, so it was very late by the time Timothy and Nono fell asleep.

As soon as the sun rose over the towers of Aunt Jessica's estate, Timothy awoke. He was astonished to find the old lady from the alley sitting by his bed. Nono was sleeping contently on her lap.

Timothy could not believe his eyes. He leapt up. "Oh, I'm so happy to see you," he cried. "I have the money I owe you." He pointed to the piles of five dollar bills.

"Oh, I don't want the money," the old woman said. "I am just happy that everything turned out right for you and that I have Nono back."

"I have made an important decision," Timothy announced.

"And what is that?"

"I shall take my money and use it to help hungry and homeless people and then . . ."

"And then?" the old woman asked.

"And then maybe you and Nono could come live with me. I mean I do owe everything to you," Timothy said.

"You don't owe me a thing," the old woman said. "But I think Nono and I could be quite happy here. Right, Nono?" Nono purred contentedly. "That small apartment in the alley was getting terribly cramped. And we still have at least one million dollars to spend. Besides, I think you are still young enough to need someone to look after you."

And that is exactly what did happen.

Timothy sold his potato for $5,000,000 to the director of the Belvedere Museum and when it was placed on display people stood in line for hours to get a glimpse of it. Tickets to see the Million Dollar Potato sold for ten to twenty dollars apiece.

Timothy and Nono and the old woman became so famous that Hollywood decided to make a movie about their lives.

And did Nono and Timothy and the old woman at the end of the alley enjoy becoming movie stars? Well, that is another story. If you remind me, I shall be glad to tell it to you. . . . Someday.

Perhaps.